George Brown, CLASS CLOWN

Return to the Scene of the Burp

For Ian, whose burps started it all!—NK

For the whole Big Burpin' Blecha Bunch!—AB

GROSSET & DUNLAP
Penguin Young Readers Group
An Imprint of Penguin Random House LLC

Text copyright © 2017 by Nancy Krulik. Illustrations copyright © 2017
by Aaron Blecha. All rights reserved. Published by Grosset & Dunlap,
an imprint of Penguin Random House LLC, 345 Hudson Street,
New York, New York 10014. GROSSET & DUNLAP is a trademark
of Penguin Random House LLC. Printed in the USA.

Library of Congress Cataloging-in-Publication Data is available.

ISBN 9780448482873   10 9 8 7 6 5 4 3 2 1

George Brown, CLASS CLOWN

Return to the Scene of the Burp

by Nancy Krulik

illustrated by Aaron Blecha

Grosset & Dunlap
An Imprint of Penguin Random House

Chapter 1

"I'm singin' in the rain . . ."

George Brown was surprised to hear his teacher, Mrs. Kelly, suddenly start **singing** in front of the class.

"I'm singin' and dancin' in the rain . . ."

The next thing George knew, Mrs. Kelly was dancing. Which wasn't nearly as surprising. **Mrs. Kelly loved to dance.** She did it all the time.

George looked up as Mrs. Kelly twirled past his desk. There were huge stains forming **under her pits**. Boy, his teacher could really sweat.

Mrs. Kelly made her way back up to the front of the room. Then she looked out at the class and tried to catch her breath.

"I bet you're wondering why I'm singing to you about rain," Mrs. Kelly said between **huffs and puffs**.

George *had* been wondering that. He'd also been wondering when his teacher would stop singing. Her voice really was awful.

"I'm singing about rain because our new science unit is **wild weather**," Mrs. Kelly continued. "And the first kind of storm we're studying is a hurricane."

George sat up in his seat. That sounded kind of interesting.

"A hurricane is a **tropical storm** that has really strong winds and heavy rain," Mrs. Kelly continued. "We rate them on a scale of one to five, depending on how hard the wind is blowing."

Max raised his hand. "Is a hurricane the same thing as a tornado?" he asked.

"No," Mrs. Kelly told him. "A tornado is actually a spinning tube of air that—"

Mrs. Kelly was busy talking about the difference between a tornado and a hurricane, but George wasn't actually listening anymore. He was too busy paying attention to the **big storm** that was brewing in the bottom of his belly.

There were bubbles in there. Hundreds of them. And not just your ordinary, run-of-the-mill **stomach bubbles**. These were *magical super burp* bubbles.

There would be trouble if those bubbles broke loose. There was *always* trouble when the **magical super burp** came around.

George's bubble trouble had started right after his family moved to Beaver Brook. George's dad was in the army, and his family moved around a lot. Which meant George had been the new kid in school lots of times. So he understood that first days could be rotten. But this first day was **the rottenest**.

At his old school, George was the class clown. But George had promised himself that things were going to be different this time. No more pranks. No more making **funny faces** behind teachers' backs.

Sadly, nobody notices a new, unfunny kid. George felt like he was invisible. Everyone ignored him. Well, everyone except Louie Farley, who for some reason had hated George from the start.

That night, George's parents took him out to Ernie's Ice Cream Emporium to cheer him up. While they were sitting outside and George was finishing his root beer float, **a shooting star** flashed across

the sky. So George made a wish.

I want to make kids laugh—but not get into trouble.

Unfortunately, the star was gone before George could finish the wish. So only half came true—the first half.

A minute later, George had a **funny feeling** in his belly. It was like there were hundreds of tiny bubbles bouncing around in there. The bubbles ping-ponged their way into his chest and bing-bonged their way up into his throat. And then . . .

George let out a big burp. A *huge* burp. A SUPER burp!

The super burp was **loud**, and it was *magic*.

Suddenly George lost control of his arms and legs. It was like they had minds of their own. His hands grabbed straws and **stuck them up his nose** like a walrus. His feet jumped up on the table and started dancing the hokey pokey. Everyone at Ernie's started laughing— except George's parents, who were covered in the ice cream he'd kicked over while he was dancing.

After that night, the burp came back over and over again. And every time it did, it made **a mess of things**.

That was why George couldn't let that burp burst out of him now. Not while Mrs. Kelly was trying to explain the difference between a hurricane and a tornado.

But the bubbles were **strong**. Already they had cling-clanged their way past his kidneys and ping-ponged their way onto his pancreas.

The bubbles slipped and slid up his spine. **They tickled at his tonsils.**

George shut his mouth tight. He had to keep the bubbles inside. The bubbles threaded their way up George's throat. They tap-danced on his tongue. And then . . .

B-U-U-U-R-P!

George let out a giant burp. A super burp. A burp so loud and so strong it could be categorized as a **catastrophic**, category-*five* burp!

"George!" Mrs. Kelly said, surprised. "What do you say?"

George wanted to say, "Excuse me." But George wasn't in charge anymore. **The burp was.** And what the burp wanted to say was, "It's a twister!"

The next thing George knew, he was leaping out of his seat. His hips were

twisting around and around.

Everyone in the class stared. An evil smile formed on Louie Farley's face.

"That **weirdo freak** is gonna get it now," Louie told his pals Mike and Max. "No way Mrs. Kelly is letting George get away with twisting around in the middle of science."

Mrs. Kelly stared at George.

George stared at Mrs. Kelly.

And then . . .

Mrs. Kelly's hips started twisting, too.

"You're right, George," Mrs. Kelly told him. "A tornado is called **a twister**. And this dance is called the twist."

Louie's smile turned upside down. He couldn't believe George wasn't in trouble.

Neither could George.

The next thing George knew, Mrs. Kelly was twisting her way down the aisle right toward him. She grabbed George's hand.

"Come on, let's do the twist," she sang as she twisted her hips.

George's face turned **beet red**. He didn't want to be dancing with his teacher. He didn't want to be holding her **sweaty, sticky hand**.

But the burp didn't mind. It just kept twisting.

George twisted up.

He twisted down.

He twisted all around. And then . . .

Pop! Suddenly something burst in the bottom of George's belly. It felt like someone had **stuck a pin** in a balloon down there. All the air rushed out of him.

The magical super burp was gone.

But George was still there. Doing the twist. And holding Mrs. Kelly's sweaty hand.

Everyone was **staring at him**.

A couple of kids were laughing. Louie was laughing the hardest.

George groaned. He was never going to live this down. Ever.

Chapter 2

"I can't believe that happened to me," George told his best friend, Alex, as they walked together over to the lunch table later that day.

"Me either," Alex agreed. "**Holding hands** with Mrs. Kelly. That had to be awful. We've really got to find a cure for that burp."

"Shhh . . . ," George whispered. "Someone will hear you."

Alex lowered his voice. "I'm working on it. There has to be **a scientific way** to get rid of a stubborn burp like the one you've got."

George was glad he had a smart friend like Alex. If anyone could find a way to **squelch the belch**, he would. Alex could figure out anything.

In fact, he'd figured out George's problem all on his own. George hadn't told Alex about the burp. He hadn't told *anyone*. It was too embarrassing.

"Hey, guys, what took you so long?" George's friend Julianna asked as she moved over to let George and Alex sit down at the lunch table.

"I was trying to find a Jell-O that didn't have a **fingerprint** on the top," George said. "I don't want to eat Jell-O some other kid touched."

"I just grabbed a banana," Alex said. "You can't **touch that** without ripping open the peel."

"That does make a banana a-peeling," Louie joked.

No one laughed. At least not until
Louie glared at Max and Mike, his best—
and only—friends.

"Good one, Louie," Max said quickly.

"Yeah, I **haven't heard that one** in a
really long time," Mike agreed. "Not since
I was five."

"I haven't heard it since I was four,"

Max said. "Maybe even three."

"You sure are funny, Louie," Mike added.

"*You* were the funny one in class this morning, *Georgie*," Sage interrupted. She **batted her eyelashes** at him.

George looked away. He hated when Sage called him *Georgie*.

"Yeah," Julianna agreed. "I can't believe you got up and did the twist **in the middle of science**."

"And held Mrs. Kelly's hand," Louie added.

"Don't remind me." George groaned.

"You crack me up," Julianna told George. "I never know when you're going to go **completely bananas**. What got into you, anyway?"

George frowned. It wasn't what had gotten into him. It was what had busted *out* of him—that darn burp. But of course George couldn't tell her that. He wasn't sure what to say.

But Louie had plenty to say. And it was all about himself. **As usual.** Louie loved talking about himself.

"All this talk about bananas reminds me that I have big news," Louie announced.

"You finally remembered you're a big, dumb, **banana-loving ape**?" George joked.

The kids all laughed. Even Max and Mike—until Louie **glared at them**.

"No," Louie said. "My big news is that my father is going to be part owner of a new ice cream parlor. And they're going to make the best banana splits in the world."

"Wow!" Sage exclaimed. "You're going to have your own **ice cream parlor**?"

"Yup," Louie replied proudly. "It's going to be called Farley's Flying Floats."

"Flying Floats?" Chris repeated. "What does that mean?"

"Just what it says," Louie told him.

"But it doesn't actually say anything," Alex told him.

"Sure it does," Louie said. "At my dad's place, your ice cream is going to **fly to your table**."

"How is it going to do that?" Max asked. "Are you going to hire birds to fly the ice cream around?"

"Won't the birds get **feathers** in the ice cream?" Mike wondered.

"Yeah," Max added. "And what about bird *poop*? That stuff goes everywhere."

Louie looked at his two friends and shook his head. "My dad's not **hiring birds**."

"Then who's going to serve the ice cream?" Max asked.

"No one," Louie replied.

George frowned. Louie was obviously dragging this out because he liked the attention. He wished he would just get to the point already.

"How can *no one* serve the ice cream?" he asked Louie.

"My dad is buying drones," Louie replied proudly.

"What's a drone?" Max asked.

"They're kind of like **flying robots**," Louie explained.

Whoa. Even George had to admit **that was cool**.

"Where's the ice cream parlor gonna be?" Chris asked Louie.

"On Main Street," Louie replied.

"But we already have an ice cream parlor on Main Street," Alex said. "Ernie's Ice Cream Emporium."

"Ernie's is yesterday's news," Louie told him. "Farley's Flying Floats is **the future**. Everyone is gonna want to hang out at my dad's place."

"But that's not fair. Your dad's restaurant could put Ernie's out of business," Alex said.

"Oh well," Louie replied with a shrug.

"Ernie has had that ice cream parlor forever," Alex continued.

"So what?" Louie said.

"So your dad already has a lot of money," Alex explained. "Why would he want to put someone **out of business**?"

Louie shrugged again. "Because he can."

George had to agree with Louie on this one—for once. He certainly didn't care if Ernie's Ice Cream Emporium went out of business. **He hated that place.** And he had every right to. After all, Ernie's was the original *scene of the burp.*

Alex knew why George hated Ernie's.

And George was Alex's best friend.

So why was he so anxious to have Ernie's Ice Cream Emporium stick around?

Chapter 3

"I don't get it," George said to Alex as the boys walked home from school at the end of the day. "**Who cares** where you buy your ice cream? A banana split is a banana split. A sundae is a sundae. A root beer float is a root beer float."

"Is it?" Alex asked George mysteriously.

George gave Alex **a funny look**. "What's that supposed to mean?"

"I just mean, what if a float isn't *just* a float?" Alex said. "What if there's **something special** about Ernie's root beer floats that gave you a super burp?"

"I told you a million times, the burp is *magic*," George insisted. "It was all because of that stupid wish I made on the shooting star."

Alex shook his head. "I'm not so sure," he said. "I don't really believe in magic. **I believe in science.** There has to be a logical reason this happened to you. That's why I keep looking for a scientific way for you to get rid of the burp."

Alex had certainly come up with lots of burp cures for George to try. Like chewing really slow. And pouring hot mustard down his throat. And drinking an **onion milkshake** . . .

So far, all George had wound up

with was gooey food, a burnt tongue, and really, really bad breath. And the super burp was still around.

"Lots of people drink Ernie's root beer floats," George pointed out. "And I'm the only one with a super burp."

"You're the only one *we know of*," Alex said. "There could be other **super burpers** out there. Maybe they don't go to our school. Or maybe they don't even go to school. Maybe they're grown-ups. Ernie's Ice Cream Emporium has been serving floats for a long, long time."

Grown-ups with a super burp problem? **Yikes.** That would be awful. Especially since some grown-ups had such important jobs.

What if the super burp made a football player get all turned around and score the winning touchdown for the other team?

Or what if the super burp made a
hairdresser go all wacko and give some
lady **a buzz cut** when she asked for a trim?

The idea that grown-ups could have
bubble trouble was **really scary**. The idea
that George could still be burping when he
was a grown-up was even scarier.

"Anyway, it would be easier for me to find a cure for the burp if I could figure out what really caused it," Alex continued. "That means knowing *all* the ingredients in Ernie's root beer float."

"That's easy," George said. "Root beer and ice cream. I like **chocolate ice cream**."

"There may be something special about Ernie's root beer. Or his ice cream," Alex said. "After all, you had other root beer floats before the day you got the burp, didn't you? Like in your old hometown."

George nodded. "Root beer floats were always **my favorite**," he said. "Not anymore!"

"We have to figure out what Ernie puts in his floats that makes them extra **gassy**," Alex said.

"How are you going to do that?"

George asked. "It's not like Ernie's gonna let some kid **wander around** his kitchen searching through his ingredients."

"I know," Alex said. "But there has to be a way for us to get back there."

"*Us?*" George's voice cracked. "I'm not going back to Ernie's. Ever. And I don't think he'd want me to."

George frowned. There were a lot of places in Beaver Brook where the shopkeepers **wouldn't want George around**. Like Mabel's Department Store, where he went up the down escalator and made a mess of  the boys' department. Or the pizza parlor, where **pizza dough** had landed on his head. Or the ice-skating rink, where . . .

"There's gotta be a way for us to get into Ernie's kitchen," Alex said, interrupting George's thoughts. *"And fast.* Before Farley's Flying Floats puts him out of business. Otherwise you could be **stuck with that burp** forever!"

Chapter 4

George couldn't believe his eyes.

Just one second ago he'd been watching *Outer Space Cowboy*, his favorite Friday night TV show. But now . . .

George was watching Louie Farley dance around in an **ice-cream cone costume**!

Louie was starring in a commercial for Farley's Flying Floats. He was wearing a giant ice-cream cone costume, topped off with a white hat with a **big red pom-pom**. George figured the pom-pom was supposed to be a cherry on top of the ice cream.

But Louie's costume wasn't the weirdest part of the commercial. The **weirdest part** came when Louie started dancing.

He moved his arms up and down. He kicked his feet from side to side. He turned around and around in a circle. When he stopped, he looked a little dizzy.

Then he started rapping.

"Chocolate, vanilla, strawberry:
topped with nuts and a big cherry.
Ice cream flies down from the sky,
with all the toppings money can buy.
So bring your dollars and your silver.

When it comes to fun, Farley's drones dilver."

That last bit made George laugh. *Dilver?* That wasn't a real word.

Louie must have meant *deliver*.

Too bad Louie hadn't realized till the end of his rap that **no actual words** rhymed with *silver*.

Rrring. Just then, George heard the phone. He hurried over and picked it up.

"Hello," George said.

"Did you just see that?" Alex asked.

"You mean Louie?" George said. "That was the **funniest thing** ever!"

"It wasn't funny at all," Alex argued.

Huh? "Were you watching the same commercial I was?" George asked. "The one where Louie was wearing that red pom-pom on his head?"

"That's the one." Alex sounded very upset.

"Don't tell me you're worried people will **make fun of Louie** for dancing around in an ice-cream cone," George said. "He's done way weirder stuff. He's *Louie*."

"I'm not worried about Louie," Alex assured George. "I'm worried about Ernie's Ice Cream Emporium. Ernie doesn't have the money to run **commercials on TV**. He can't compete with Farley's."

"You'd think with all that money, Mr. Farley could have hired **a better rapper** than Louie," George said.

"This isn't about Louie," Alex reminded him. "It's about Ernie keeping his business. And about *finding you a burp cure*. Which is why I figured out a way for us to **get into Ernie's kitchen** to look at the ingredients."

"How?" George asked. "Are we going to sneak in a window?"

"Nope," Alex said. "We don't have to sneak in at all. I can go in the kitchen at Ernie's anytime I want. **I work there.**"

"You work there?" George asked. "Since when?"

"Since tonight, when I asked Ernie if I could help him out by sweeping and setting up the tables on Saturday mornings," Alex replied.

"Oh, kind of like what I do at Mr. Furstman's pet shop," George said.

"Exactly," Alex said. "**So here's the plan.** Tomorrow, you come over to Ernie's early in the morning—before you go to the pet shop. I'll let you in."

"Won't Ernie mind if you let someone in before his ice cream parlor opens?" George wondered. "Especially if that someone is me?"

"Ernie told me he does paperwork

in his office in the morning," Alex said. "I'll be the only one in the front of the restaurant. **We're free to investigate.** Ernie will never know you were there."

Investigate. George liked the sound of that. It made it seem like he and Alex were **kid detectives** on a big case.

Which they kind of were.

The Case of the Baffling Burp.

THE CASE OF THE BAFFLING BURP

Chapter 5

Tap. Tap. Tap.

Early the next morning, George **knocked on the glass door** at Ernie's Ice Cream Emporium. Alex hurried to let him in.

"Perfect timing," Alex whispered. "Ernie's got the office door closed. He'll never know you're here—as long as we're quiet."

"Oh, I will be," George said. "I don't want to get in trouble for **snooping around** where I don't belong. Especially since Ernie hates me."

"He doesn't hate you," Alex said. "He probably doesn't even remember what happened that night."

"How could he forget?" George asked. "It's not every day someone jumps up onto a table and does **the hokey pokey**."

Alex didn't answer. George figured that was because he knew George was right.

"Here, put this on." Alex pulled two hats out of his backpack and handed one to George.

George looked at the hat. It looked sort of like a baseball cap, except it had a brim in the front *and* in the back.

"What kind of hat is this?" George asked Alex.

"**A detective hat**," Alex told him. "Like the one Sherlock Holmes used to wear."

"Sherlock who?" George asked.

"Sherlock Holmes," Alex repeated. "He was a famous detective. He solved all kinds of mysteries. Wearing these hats will **give us inspiration**."

George didn't need any extra inspiration when it came to solving this mystery. But he put the hat on, anyway.

Alex handed George a big magnifying glass. "You'll need this, too," he said. "Some of those ingredient labels are hard to read."

George held the magnifying glass up near his eye. Suddenly he was face-to-face with a **giant cockroach**.

"Ernie's got to clean this place more often," he told Alex.

"Don't worry about that," Alex said. "Just get looking."

"What am I looking for?" George asked.

"I don't know," Alex admitted. "Any **weird ingredient** you've never heard of."

George opened the refrigerator. There were bottles and bottles of cold root beer piled up in there. He held the magnifying glass up to one of the labels.

"Cherry tree bark?" George read. **"There's tree bark in root beer?"**

Alex nodded. "A lot of them have that. I doubt you're allergic, because you probably drank root beer with cherry tree bark plenty of times before the burp. Same for **sassafras**. It's found in lots of root beer, too."

George laughed. "*Sassafras*. That's a funny word."

"It's a tree that's pretty common," Alex said. "Especially here in . . ."

Alex kept talking about sassafras, but

George couldn't pay attention to what he was saying. Not while there were so many **sassy bubbles** bouncing around in his belly.

Already the bubbles had cling-clanged past his kidneys and ping-ponged their way onto his pancreas.

Uh-oh! The burp was back!

Roing. Rong. The bubbles ripped through George's ribs.

Boing. Bong. They bounced up his backbone.

George zipped his lips. Tight. The bubbles were strong. But he was stronger. If he could just keep them from bursting out . . .

The bubbles tickled his trachea. They trampled his tongue. They . . .

George let out a burp so loud, and so powerful, it shook the leaves of sassafras trees for miles around and sent his hat flying.

"Dude, no!" Alex exclaimed.

Dude, yes! **The super burp was free.** And now, whatever the burp wanted to do, George had to do.

The first thing the burp wanted to do was play with whipped cream. So the next thing George knew, he was **spraying whipped cream** all over himself.

He made himself a whipped-cream beard.

And a whipped-cream bracelet.

And a whipped-cream crown that went all the way around his head.

"Cut it out!" Alex grabbed the whipped-cream container from George's hands.

But the burp didn't want to cut it out. It wanted to shout.

So George shouted, "I scream. You scream. We all scream for ice cream!"

George's feet ran toward the giant freezer. He flung the door open and raced inside.

George opened a huge container of ice cream. He **scooped out a handful** of vanilla and rolled it into a ball.

"Ice-cream-ball fight!" George shouted.

"Dude, cut it out," Alex said. "You're gonna **get me fired**."

George threw the ice-cream ball at Alex's head.

"What's going on in here?!" Ernie yelled as he raced into the kitchen.

Slam! Alex shut the freezer door. Now George was alone in the **freezing-cold room**.

Well, not *all* alone. The burp was in there with him.

But burps aren't very good company. And they don't usually **stick around** when they get caught.

Pop! At just that moment, something burst in the bottom of George's belly. It felt like someone had stuck a pin in a balloon down there. All the air rushed out of him.

The magical super burp was gone.

But George was in the freezer.

Covered in whipped cream.

George knew Alex had locked him in the freezer so Ernie wouldn't know he was there. Which was a really nice thing for his friend to do.

But it was really cold in the freezer.

George's eyes were watering. **His nose was leaking.** His teeth were chattering. George couldn't stay in there **much longer**.

"Hey, let me out of here!" George shouted. He banged on the freezer door.

Finally, the door opened. George came face-to-face with Ernie. Well, face-to-*belt*, anyway. Ernie was pretty tall.

"You again!" Ernie shouted angrily. "What are you doing in my freezer?"

Gulp. George didn't know what to say.

"He was helping me clean up," Alex told Ernie quickly. "But he saw a cockroach, and he **freaked out**. He locked himself in the freezer to get away from the roach."

Alex wasn't exactly lying. That was sort of true. Only the cockroach hadn't caused the freak-out. **The burp had.**

Just the *word* cockroach was enough to freak *Ernie* out. "We can't have roaches!" he exclaimed. "Alex, we have to really scrub this kitchen. Now."

"I'll get right on it," Alex said.

"Good." Ernie turned to George. "And you get out of here. I have **enough problems** with the new ice cream parlor across the street. I don't need the added worry that something bad might happen to you here."

George frowned. *Might* happen? Something bad had already happened to George in this ice cream parlor. The burp had struck there—*twice.*

Ernie didn't have to worry about George **sticking around**. There was no way George was waiting for the burp's third strike. Because everybody knew what happened after three strikes.

You were out.

Which was right where George was headed. *Out the door.*

And fast.

Chapter 6

That night, George sat and stared at the e-vite on his computer screen. He couldn't believe it. Louie was inviting George to be his guest at his dad's ice cream parlor on Sunday afternoon? **How weird.** Louie never invited George to anything.

At least, not unless he had to.

And the Farleys never gave anything away for free. This had to be **a gag**.

George hurried to the phone to call Alex.

"Hey, Alex," George said. "Did you just get an e-vite from Louie?"

"Yeah," Alex replied. "But I'm not going to have ice cream at that place."

"But it's free," George said. He paused

for a moment. "I wonder why Mr. Farley is giving away **free ice cream**."

"Word-of-mouth advertising," Alex replied. "If a bunch of kids like the ice cream, they'll come back with their parents. And they'll tell other kids."

"That's pretty smart," George said.

"It's pretty *sneaky*," Alex told him. "Ernie's is usually **packed** on Sundays. But tomorrow every kid we know will be at Farley's. Except us of course."

"What do you mean *us*?" George asked. **"I'm going."**

"But you hate Louie," Alex said.

Alex had a point. Still . . .

"I never turn down free ice cream," George finally said. "Even if I have to **put up with Louie** to get it."

Putting up with Louie wasn't easy. Especially when he was bragging.

"This is going to be the most **popular place** in all of Beaver Brook," Louie boasted as he sat at the head of a long table at Farley's Flying Floats on Sunday afternoon. "Soon you won't be able to get in without waiting on a **really long line**."

George looked around the room. The fourth-graders were sitting at Louie's table. There was a long table of middle-school kids sitting with Louie's big brother, Sam. Another table was filled with Louie's parents and their friends. The place was **definitely crowded**. Then again, they *were* giving away *free ice cream.*

"When's our ice cream coming?" Chris asked Louie. "I'm hungry."

"Me too," Julianna agreed. "I can practically taste that banana split."

"It takes a long time to make the perfect banana split," Louie said. "But in the meantime, check out this new **remote-control race car** my mom bought me."

Louie reached down and pulled a model car from under the table. The car was bright red and had the number one painted on its side.

George had to admit that was one nice car. George loved remote-control cars. And he would have liked to have one just like that. But George would have had to spend **his own money** to get it. Louie's mom just gave it to him.

"You should see this thing turn corners," Louie said as he grabbed the remote control.

But before Louie could turn the car on, Max started **bouncing up and down** in his seat.

"Look!" he shouted. **"Here come the drones!"**

"I saw that drone first," Mike told him. "I just didn't say anything."

"You did not!" Max said.

"Did too," Mike argued.

A drone flew up beside Julianna. She reached over and took her **banana split**.

"Hey!" she exclaimed. "There's no banana in here."

"I guess the banana split," George joked.

"I only got **six sprinkles** on my sundae," Sage said. "I get hundreds of sprinkles when I'm at Ernie's."

Louie scowled. "Didn't anyone ever teach you not to complain when you're getting something for free?" he asked Sage and Julianna. "Besides, you gotta admit **the drones are cool**."

"They are," Julianna admitted.

"At least the ice cream is good," Sage said. "Although it's hard to mess up vanilla."

Louie smiled. "So, anyway, as I was saying," he continued as he turned on his remote-control car. "You should see how this thing takes corners. It's amazing!"

Louie pushed a button on the remote control. The engine on his toy car **revved up**.

Then he pushed
another button and—
Splat! One of the
drones flipped over on its

side, dropping
a chocolate-
marshmallow ice
cream sundae
**right on Chris's
head**.

"Hey!" Chris
shouted. "I have a
marshmallow in my ear."

"Pull it out," George told him.

"What?" Chris asked. "I can't hear you
with this **marshmallow in my ear**."

Splash! Another drone turned and
spilled a whole root beer float on Max's lap.

"What's wrong with the drones?"
Julianna wondered.

"It's Louie's remote control," George

said. "It's making the drones go **all crazy**."

"That's impossible," Louie said angrily.

"No, it's not," George argued. "I was reading about drones online last night. Some of the cheaper ones work by regular toy remote controls. These must be that kind."

Louie's face turned bright red. It almost looked like **steam was coming out of his ears**. "Are you saying my dad's cheap?" he demanded.

Splunk. A drone zoomed around the corner and dumped a big strawberry sundae on Sage's lap.

"Oh no!" Sage shouted. "My new dress."

"Louie! Turn that thing off," Julianna shouted.

"I'm trying!" Louie said. He began

frantically pushing buttons on his remote.

But the more buttons Louie pushed, the crazier the drones got.

Two of them **crashed in midair**. Ice cream rained down from above.

"Mmmm . . . pistachio," Julianna said as she scooped **a big glob** of green ice cream off her lap and into her mouth.

George opened his mouth just in time to catch a cherry.

"Good one," Julianna told him.

"Thanks," George replied.

Louie's mother came racing over to the table. She stopped right in front of George and glared at him.

"What's going on here, George Brown?" she demanded.

George frowned. Mrs. Farley always thought that everything that went wrong was **George's fault**. Not that he blamed her. After all, it usually *was* his fault.

But not this time.

"Louie's remote control is making all the drones go nuts," George told her.

"*Wet* nuts," Julianna said as a big glob of nuts landed on Mike's head. "Real ones."

"Louie!" Mrs. Farley shouted. "Turn that thing off."

"I'm trying, Mom," Louie said, frantically **pushing more buttons** on the remote.

"Pull the batteries out," George told him.

"Why should I listen to you?" Louie demanded.

"Because he's right," said Louie's big brother, Sam. He leaped up from his seat, **yanked the remote** from Louie's hands, and pulled out the batteries.

"Dad told you not to bring that **stupid toy** with you today," Sam grumbled.

Louie looked like he was about to cry.

The drones turned in midair and went back into the kitchen. Everyone just sat there, **covered in ice cream**—and stared at Louie.

"Lou Lou Poo!" Mrs. Farley exclaimed. "What have you done?"

"But . . . I . . . It wasn't my fault," Louie stammered. "The remote **went wacko**."

George grinned. It was fun watching someone else get in trouble for a change. Especially when that someone was Louie Farley.

Chapter 7

"It was hilarious," George told Alex later that afternoon, while the boys were hanging out in George's living room. "Mrs. Farley had this **big glop** of chocolate sauce hanging off her nose. Just hanging there. Like a **chocolate booger**."

Alex laughed. "That had to be really funny."

"It was," George said. "I guess Mr. Farley's plan for getting kids psyched up for his ice cream parlor didn't work too well."

"Not *this* plan, anyway," Alex agreed. "But you know the Farley family. They're bound to come up with some other **sneaky way** to get everyone to go to their place instead of Ernie's. Which is why we have to find out what caused your burp as fast as we can—just in case Ernie's Ice Cream Emporium really does go out of business."

"It was pretty empty in there today, huh?" George asked.

Alex nodded. "I think Ernie was actually crying in his office at one point. **His eyes were all red.**"

Wow. George had never seen a grown-up cry before.

"Were you able to look at any more ingredients after I left yesterday?" George asked Alex.

"There's nothing out of the ordinary in Ernie's root beer floats," Alex told him.

"That's why I keep telling you the **burp is magic**," George said. "It was that dumb shooting star."

"I'm not so sure," Alex told him. "I still think there's a scientific explanation. And I may have figured out a way to **solve this mystery**."

George sat up excitedly. "You have? What is it? Tell me!"

"I don't know if you're gonna like it," Alex said.

"Oh, come on," George insisted. "It can't be any worse than **spicy ginger** candy or drinking gallons and gallons of warm water or—"

"This plan's a little different," Alex told him. "You're gonna have to return to the scene of the burp."

"I'm gonna have to *what*?" George asked.

"Return to the scene of the burp," Alex repeated. "They do it all the time in **mystery books**. The police make everyone reenact the crime exactly as it happened. That's when the real criminal gets revealed."

"What criminal?" George wondered. "My problem is a burp."

"In this case, the burp is the **real troublemaker**. The thing that caused all your problems in the first place," Alex told him.

"Well," George admitted, "I guess

when you put it that way . . ."

"I'm gonna be there, watching everything," Alex assured him. "I want to see if there's anything weird that happens when you wish on a shooting star. Anything out of the ordinary that might give us a clue about how the burp got into you. Then we can use that information to help us get the burp out of you."

"The burp gets out of me all the time," George reminded him. "That's the problem."

"You know what I mean," Alex said.

"But what if wishing again makes things worse?" George asked him.

"How much worse can it get?" Alex replied.

That was true.

"Okay. So you and your folks come to Ernie's tomorrow night," Alex said.

"You order the same root beer float, and you make **the same wish**."

"Tomorrow?" George asked nervously. "Ernie is still mad at me from *yesterday*. Can't we wait a week?"

"Nope," Alex said. "I saw in the newspaper that there's going to be a **meteor shower** tomorrow night. That means lots of shooting stars. You have to sit at the same table and make the same wish. Everything has to be **exactly the same**."

But George knew everything wasn't going to be exactly the same. It couldn't be. Because now, wherever George went and whatever he did, the burp was with him. **Just waiting** to cause as much bubble trouble as it possibly could.

Chapter 8

"Can we sit outside?" George asked his mom and dad as they walked over to Ernie's Ice Cream Emporium Monday night. **"I want to see the sky."**

That wasn't exactly the truth. But it wasn't like George could tell them about the whole return-to-the-scene-of-the-burp thing—especially since he hadn't told them about the burp in the first place.

"I'm surprised you wanted more ice cream after yesterday," George's mom said. "It took me an hour to get the **chocolate sauce** out of your shirt."

"I'm really in the mood for a root beer float," George told her. Which wasn't exactly the truth, either.

"We better make this fast," George's dad said as they sat down. "It's almost nineteen hundred hours and you still have homework."

George knew nineteen hundred hours was seven o'clock at night in army-talk. **It was getting dark.** If everything went according to plan, there would be a shooting star overhead soon.

"It's not really crowded here tonight, is it?" George's mom said as she looked at the menu.

"**A lot of people** are at Farley's Flying Floats," George's dad pointed out, looking across the street.

There was definitely a line outside Farley's. But at least Ernie's wasn't completely empty. There were people sitting at a few of the tables.

In fact, George recognized some of Sam Farley's middle-school friends sitting with their parents. He guessed they didn't like having ice cream **dumped on their heads** yesterday.

"Oh look, there's Alex," George's mom said. "I wonder why he's wearing that funny hat."

George looked over at a stool near the counter. Alex was wearing his **Sherlock Holmes hat** and taking notes on a pad, just like a real detective on TV.

"He's all alone," George's mom continued. "You should go ask him to join us."

"We can't ask him to sit here," George said quickly.

"Why not?" his mom asked.

The real reason George couldn't invite Alex to join them was because everything had to be exactly the same as it had been **that first night** when the burp arrived. Alex hadn't been sitting with them then. So he couldn't sit with them now.

But George couldn't say that. So instead he answered, "Alex works here. I don't think he's supposed to sit with the customers."

Before George's mom could reply, a waitress came **roller-skating** over to George's table.

"Hi," the waitress greeted them.
"What can I get for you folks?"

"I'll have a root beer float," George
said. "With **two scoops** of chocolate ice
cream."

That was exactly what he had ordered
when he and his family had come there
before.

"I'll have **vanilla ice cream** with
chocolate sauce," George's mom told the
waitress.

George smiled. That was exactly what his mom had ordered the last time they were all at Ernie's. Perfect.

"And I'll have a banana split with—" George's dad began.

"No, you can't have that!" George shouted suddenly.

"Why not?" his dad asked him.

"Um . . . well . . . because you always like rocky road ice cream sundaes," George said. "Why don't you get one of those?"

"Tonight I want a banana split," his dad explained.

"Come on, Dad, you know you want that sundae," George said. "I bet they'll put **three cherries** on it if you ask them for it."

George's dad gave him a strange look. Then he said, "Okay. That actually sounds pretty good."

Phew. For a minute there, George thought his dad was going to order the wrong thing. That could have **ruined** everything.

"Okay, I'll get your order for you right away," the waitress said.

As the waitress skated off, George **looked up at the sky**. It was really dark now. Those shooting stars would probably arrive soon.

So would George's root beer float. Everything was in place.

There was nothing left to do but wait.

Chapter 9

"Here you go," the waitress said as she placed the root beer float in front of George. "Drink up."

George started feeling **really nervous** as the scent of chocolate and root beer wafted up toward his nose. He hadn't had a root beer float in a long time. Not since . . .

"Hey! Look up!" George's mom shouted suddenly. "It's a shooting star. Quick. **Make a wish.**"

George wanted to tell the star to wait. He wasn't ready. He hadn't even taken a single sip of his root beer float—the way he had that fateful night.

But there was no time. Shooting stars move too fast. And you can't stop them. George was going to have to make his wish . . . again. Right now.

"I want to make kids laugh—but not get into trouble," George whispered quietly.

And with that, **the star was gone**.

George sat there. Waiting. He wasn't sure what he was waiting for. But he figured something would happen. After all, he'd just made the same wish, at the same table, with the same star overhead. Well, maybe not the same star. But a shooting star, anyway. And now . . .

Nothing was happening. Nothing at all.

George looked over at Alex.

Alex shrugged. He wrote something in his little note pad.

George put a hand on his belly. Nope.

No bubbles there.

"Aren't you going to have your float?" George's mom asked him. "Your chocolate ice cream is **going to melt**."

"Um . . . sure," George said. He picked up his long, skinny spoon and dug it into the ice cream. He opened his mouth and then . . .

Splish-splash. Flish-flash.

Suddenly, George felt something move **inside his belly**.

Ping-pong. Bing-bong.

Uh-oh. There were bubbles in there. Hundreds of them. The super burp was back.

The bubbles were bombarding George's bladder. They were leaping on his liver.

"What's wrong, soldier?" George's dad asked him. "Is there a problem with the float?"

George couldn't answer his dad. That would mean opening his mouth—and then the burp might slip out.

The bubbles were moving really, really fast. They thrashed at George's throat. They licked at his lips. They . . .

George let out a burp. A big burp. A *super* burp. A burp so loud and so strong it **made the table shake**.

"George, what do you say?" his mother asked, surprised.

George wanted to say excuse me. But George **wasn't in charge** any more. The burp was. And what the burp wanted to say was:

"GOOD EVENING, LADIES AND GERMS!"

The next thing he knew, George had jumped up out of his seat. Everyone at Ernie's turned to stare. "**Stand down, soldier**," George's dad ordered. "Take a seat."

But the burp didn't want to stand down. The burp wanted to tell jokes.

"Do you know how to make an **elephant float**?" George loudly asked his mother.

George's mother just stared at him with surprise.

"Drop two scoops of elephant into some root beer," George said.

Two little kids at the next table started to laugh.

George hurried to their table. "Do you know what you call a **flying monkey**?" he asked the kids.

"No, what?" one of them replied.

"A hot air baboon!" George shouted.

The kids laughed harder. So did a bunch of teenagers nearby. So George raced over to them.

"How do bees **brush their hair**?" he asked one of the teenagers.

"How?" she wondered.

"With a honey comb!" George answered.

Now everyone at Ernie's was laughing—even George's parents. And the burp still had more jokes to tell.

"Why did the duck cross the road?"

George asked two old ladies who were sipping coffee in the corner.

"Why?" one of them said.

"It was the chicken's day off!" George replied.

"You're a very **funny boy**," the old lady told George.

George turned to a man with a long red beard and a big mustache. "Do you know who shaves **ten times a day** and still has a beard?" he asked.

The man shook his head.

"A barber!" George said.

People were laughing really hard now. And then . . .

Pop! Suddenly, George felt something burst in the bottom of his belly. All the air **rushed out of him**. The super burp was gone. But George was still there. In the middle of Ernie's. Surrounded by a bunch of laughing people.

Huh?

There were no broken dishes.

No messes to clean up.

And nobody was angry with him. Not even his parents.

The burp had struck at Ernie's a third time. But no one was throwing George out.

George couldn't believe it. This couldn't be real.

George held out his arm. "**Somebody pinch me**," he said.

PINCH!

One of the teenagers gave George's arm a good, hard pinch.

"Ow!" George cried out.

That settled it.

This was no dream.

It was a *dream come true.*

Chapter 10

"Last night was one strange night," George remarked as he and Alex walked onto the school playground the next morning. "I didn't even get a chance to **drink a sip** of my root beer float before the burp hit again. So we're no closer to finding out what caused it."

"We're a little closer," Alex disagreed. "Now we know that the root beer float **didn't cause** your burp."

"*I've* been telling you that," George insisted. "The burp is magic. So the cure will have to be magic, too."

Alex shook his head. "And I keep telling *you* that there's no such thing as magic."

"Well, at least I didn't **get in trouble** this time," George said. "That's really something."

"Maybe the burp is mellowing," Alex suggested.

"Can burps do that?" George asked.

Alex opened his mouth to answer. But before he could say a word, **a loud shout** came from the other end of the playground.

"Oh, *Georgie*!"

It was Sage. She was running toward them, with Chris and Julianna right behind.

"Why didn't you tell me you were doing **your act** last night?" Sage asked George. "I would have been there to cheer you on. My cousin Willow was at Ernie's.

even rhyme," he told Louie.

Louie ignored him. "And then I did this really cool **tap dance**," he said. "I kicked my legs to the front. Then I kicked them back and . . . Whoops!"

Louie tripped over his shoelace and **landed on his butt**.

George started to laugh.

"I don't know how you missed my commercial," Louie said as he scrambled to his feet. "My dad ran it on every channel last night. **It cost a fortune.** But advertising is important."

"*Georgie* missed your commercial because he was doing his stand-up comedy act at Ernie's," Sage said.

Louie gave George a look. "Ernie's?

Nobody goes there anymore. Nobody cool, anyway." He laughed. "Then again, you're not cool."

"Are you kidding?" Sage asked Louie. "Georgie is so cool he could **freeze the sun**." She smiled at George. "You can use that in your act if you want."

George frowned. The joke was pretty dumb. He'd never use that in his act—if he actually had an act. **Which he didn't.** It was the super burp that was doing all the joking around last night.

BRRRRIIIIINNNNGGG! Just then, the bell rang.

As the kids headed into the school, George gave Alex **a funny look**. "You got pretty quiet out there," he told Alex.

"I was thinking," Alex said.

"About what?" George asked.

"An idea I had," Alex replied **mysteriously**. "I'll tell you all about it—as soon as I have everything figured out."

"You want me to WHAT?" George

shouted into the phone
that evening.

"I want you to go
back to Ernie's Ice
Cream Emporium,"
Alex repeated calmly.

"No, thanks,"
George said. "I'm
lucky I didn't get in
trouble Sunday night

when **the burp burst**. Right
now, nobody at Ernie's is
mad at me. But I can't
guarantee what will
happen if I go back there
again. I haven't always
been **so lucky** when the
burp burst out there."

"Come on," Alex pleaded. "Ernie's a nice guy. And he's gonna lose his business—but maybe not if you help him."

"What do you mean?" George asked.

"Ernie thinks he could get a lot of customers if he started an **open-mike night**," Alex explained.

"So get Mike to tell jokes," George said. "Get Max, too."

George was only kidding. He knew open mike was really a kind of **talent show**. He just didn't want to be a part of it.

Alex laughed. "See, you're really funny," he said.

"Seriously. What does Ernie need me for?" George asked.

"**Everyone's talking** about what happened at Ernie's Ice Cream Emporium last night," Alex told him. "You've got star power now. People will come just to see you."

Star power? Wow. Nobody had ever called

George a star before.

Besides, Alex was his best friend. This was the least George could do.

"Well," George finally said. "I guess if you think it could bring **a lot of customers** into Ernie's, I could tell a few jokes."

"I do," Alex assured him. "And if he gets enough customers back, maybe Farley's Flying Floats will have to close."

"That would be the end of those awful Louie commercials," George thought out loud.

"Yep," Alex agreed. "We can save Ernie's Ice Cream Emporium and give Louie one less thing to **brag about**—if everything goes as planned."

George frowned. That was a very big *if*.

Especially with the magical super burp still **lurking around**. There was no telling what might happen if *that* decided to burst out and be part of the show.

Chapter 11

"Look!" George's mother exclaimed as they walked into Ernie's Ice Cream Emporium on Saturday night. "Your picture is on **that poster**, George!"

George had worried for a long time about seeing his picture on a poster. He always imagined the signs would say:

GEORGE BROWN: WANTED FOR BUBBLE TROUBLE

But *this* poster didn't say anything like that. It said:

OPEN-MIKE NIGHT AT ERNIE'S ICE CREAM EMPORIUM.

DISCOVER THE BEST TALENT IN TOWN.

LIKE THIS FUNNY MAN, GEORGE BROWN!

BE PART OF THE SHOW, AND ENJOY OUR TASTY
TREATS.

As George walked into the restaurant,
Alex came running over. "There you are," he
said. "I thought maybe you'd **chickened out**."

"I almost did," George admitted.

"My mom saved you guys seats," Alex
said. "She's down in front."

"Is your mom going to let you eat ice
cream tonight?" George asked Alex.

"As long as I go right into the bathroom
to **brush my teeth** afterward," Alex said.

George wasn't surprised. Alex's mom
was a dentist. She was always making him
brush his teeth in weird places.

"You're on first," Alex told him. "Are you
nervous?"

"Yeah," George admitted. "But not about
telling jokes."

"Oh," Alex said. "You're worried the
burp will come out again, huh?"

George shook his head. "I've got bigger problems. **My dad wants to perform.**"

"What talent does he have?" Alex asked

George shook his head. "I have no idea. He says it's a surprise."

"Oh no," Alex said. "A parental surprise. That's never good."

"I know," George agreed. "And practically **the whole fourth grade** is here to see it."

Just then, Ernie stood up in the middle of the restaurant. "Welcome to our first open-mike night," he said. "It's good to see all of you again."

The crowd cheered.

George gulped.

"Ladies and gentlemen," Ernie continued. "I give you our first act: George Brown, Town Clown!"

George walked up and took the microphone. "Hello, Beaver Brook!" he said, trying to sound like a real **stand-up comic**.

He walked over to the table where Alex's mom and his parents were sitting. "Do you know what instrument is found in the bathroom?" he asked Alex's mom.

"No, what?" Alex's mom wondered.

"A *tuba* toothpaste!" George exclaimed.

Alex's mom laughed. "I love a good **tooth joke**," she said.

George headed over to Sage and Julianna. "What do you get if you mix a parrot with a shark?"

"What?" Julianna asked.

"A bird that can **chew your ear off**!" George replied.

"Oh, *Georgie*, you're so funny." Sage giggled.

George turned to Chris. "What do you call a painting by a cat?" he asked him.

"I don't know," Chris said.

"A *paw*-trait!" George told him.

Chris laughed so hard, **he snorted**.

Everyone was laughing—and not because the burp had made George do anything goofy. *Wow!* George was having so much fun he didn't want to sit down.

But eventually Ernie came and took the microphone. It was time to give someone else a turn.

Unfortunately, that someone else was **George's dad**.

"What's your talent?" Ernie asked him.

"I'm a singer," George's dad said.

"I didn't know your father could sing," Alex said.

"He can't," George and his mother both said at the exact same time.

George's dad clicked an app on his phone. **Music started to play.** Then George's dad began to sing—badly.

"First to fight for the right." George's dad's voice cracked, but he kept singing. *"And to build the nation's might."*

"What song is this?" Alex asked George.

"The US Army's official song. It's pretty much the **only song** he knows." George buried his head in his hands. "He sings worse than Mrs. Kelly. Can

this get any more embarrassing?"

George's dad began to march around the ice cream parlor. He **saluted** each table as he passed by.

"I guess it *can* get more embarrassing," George groaned.

A group of kids got up out of their seats.

"Oh man, he's **chasing away** the customers," George groaned.

Except, the kids didn't leave. They started marching behind George's dad. And the few that knew the words started singing, too.

Wow! The kids didn't think George's dad was weird. **They thought he was cool.** Which George had to admit he was—at least as cool as a grown-up could be, anyway.

"If you can't beat 'em, join 'em," George said. He leaped out of his chair to **join the marchers**.

"*Count off,*" George's dad sang.

"*Hup, two, three, four,*" George counted loudly.

As he marched past the outdoor tables, George glanced across the street. The mayor and his wife were walking into

Farley's Flying Floats with a bunch of other important-looking people.

Bummer.

Getting rid of Ernie's competition wasn't going to be as easy as he and Alex had hoped. It would take a whole army of customers to beat out Mr. Farley and his **rich, fancy friends**.

Still, George knew Alex wasn't going to give up. That was just the kind of kid he was. So George wasn't going to give up, either.

"And we'll fight with all our might," George sang out loudly. *"As the army keeps rolling along."*

Chapter 12

"Do you think Ernie will be able to stay in business after last night?" George asked Alex as the boys walked along Main Street the next morning. They were on the way to George's mom's craft store, the Knit Wit, to take a **tie-dyeing class**.

"I don't know," Alex admitted. "It depends on if all those people will come back over and over again."

"I just hope he doesn't do another open-mike night," George said. "Some of those acts were **pretty bad**."

"I still can't believe my mom actually got up and showed everyone the correct way to floss." Alex groaned. "That was really embarrassing."

"I can't argue with you there," George agreed sympathetically. He looked up. "Hey! What's **that crane** doing in front of Farley's Flying Floats?"

"I have no idea," Alex replied. "Let's go check it out."

The boys reached the ice cream parlor just in time to see the *F* in *Farley's* being **taken down** by the crane.

"Stay out of the way, boys," a workman said. "Those letters are heavy."

"Why are you taking the letters down?" Alex asked.

"This place is **going out of business**," the workman told him.

"Wow!" George exclaimed. "Ernie only had one open-mike night, and already Mr. Farley realized he'd lost all his customers."

"That's not why," the workman told him. "One of those drones spilled a malt on the mayor's wife's head. **Knocked her wig clear off.** Now the mayor's banned drones on Main Street."

"No drones, no flying floats," Alex said.

The workman nodded.

"I don't think Mr. Farley would pay waiters to serve ice cream," Alex continued. "He's too cheap."

"I guess Ernie didn't need an open-mike night to drive Farley's out of business," George said. "What a waste of time."

"It wasn't a waste," Alex told him. "You got through a whole night of making people laugh **without a single burp**."

"That's true," George agreed. "I've been burp-free for almost two whole days. Maybe the super burp's finally moved on."

"I hope so." Alex glanced down at his watch. "*We* better move on. We don't want to be late for your mom's class."

George took one more look at the sign over Farley's Flying Floats. Only now it said RLEY'S FLYING FLOATS. The *F* and *A* were already gone.

Now, if only the **magical super burp** would stay *fa, fa* away. Then everything would be perfect.

"This is a very expensive white T-shirt," Louie told George and the other kids while they waited for the tie-dyeing class to begin. "But my mother said **I could dye it.** We can always buy me another one."

George stared at Louie's expensive T-shirt. **It didn't look any different** than the one his mother had gotten him at the dollar store.

"*Georgie,* you were so funny last night," Sage said, ignoring Louie completely.

"Hilarious," Julianna agreed.

"I laughed so hard **I snorted**," Chris added.

"I heard you," George said with a grin. "*Everyone* heard you."

Chris laughed—and snorted—again.

"Okay, kids," George's mom called out. "Let's get started. I'm going to show you how to wrap your rubber bands around your shirts. Then we can **dunk them** in those big vats of dye. We have lots of great colors—red, yellow, green . . ."

Bing-bong. Ping-pong.

George's mom was still talking, but George couldn't concentrate on what she was saying. He **couldn't concentrate** on anything except—

Cling-clang. Fling-flang.

The magical super burp! **It was back.** And it was going crazy.

The bubbles ricocheted off George's ribcage.

They charged through his chest.

They ganged up on his gums. And then . . .

 **B-U-U-U-R-P!**

The bubbles burst right out of him.

"Dude, no!" Alex whispered.

Dude, yes! The burp had escaped. And now George had to do whatever the burp wanted him to do.

And what the burp wanted to do was **go barefoot**. So the next thing George knew, he was kicking off his shoes and throwing off his socks.

"George!" his mother exclaimed. "Put your shoes back on!"

George wanted to put his shoes back on. But the burp had other plans.

"This **little piggy** went to market," George said, pulling on his big toe. "This little piggy stayed home. This . . ."

Louie pinched his nose. "Your feet **stink like smelly cheese**," he told George.

"Little piggy had none," George continued. "And this little piggy—"

When George reached the last little piggy, he ran, ran, ran . . . all the way to a big vat of purple dye. *Then he jumped right in.*

Purple dye splashed everywhere.

"Splish, splash, I'm taking a bath!"
George shouted, rubbing purple dye
under his pits like he was taking a
shower. "Rub a dub du—"

Pop! Suddenly, George felt something burst in the bottom of his belly. All the air rushed out of him.

The magical super burp was gone.

But George was still there—standing **in a vat of purple dye**.

"Look at this mess!" George's mother exclaimed. "What do you have to say for yourself?"

George opened his mouth to say, "I'm sorry." And that's exactly what came out.

"I don't know why you do things like this," his mom said with a sigh.

George climbed out of the vat of dye. He started heading **toward the bathroom**.

"Where are you going?" his mother asked him.

"To wash my feet off," George replied.

"Don't bother," his mom told him. "The dye is going to have to **wear off**.

And that could take a while."

"You mean I'm stuck with **purple piggies**—er—I mean, *toes*?" George asked.

"For now," his mother said. "I'm just glad I put newspaper down on the floor. This could have been worse."

George looked at his feet. *Worse?* He couldn't imagine how. Purple toes were about as bad as it got.

"You know, *Georgie*," Sage said, **batting her eyelashes** up and down. "Purple is my favorite color. I like your little piggies."

Oh brother.

Louie laughed. "I love when she calls him *Georgie*," he told Max and Mike.

George groaned.

Alex gave George an encouraging smile. "Don't worry," he whispered. "I'm not giving up on finding a cure. A good detective **never gives up** on a tough case."

And neither does a good friend, George thought. He sure was lucky to have a friend like Alex.

Especially since he had one more favor to ask of him.

"Maybe while you're at it, you could find a way to get rid of Louie, too," George asked Alex. "He's **as big of a pain** as a super burp."

Well, that wasn't exactly fair.

The super burp definitely caused George a lot of trouble. And if his purple toes were an indication, it **wasn't mellowing** at all.

Still, there had been that one amazing night at Ernie's when the burp had helped

George make people laugh—and nothing bad had happened.

And there was always the possibility it might happen again. So maybe the burp wasn't all bad.

But nothing good *ever* happened when Louie was around. **He was just rotten.**

And George didn't think there was any possibility that would ever change.

"Actually, Louie's *worse* than the magical super burp," George corrected himself. "And that's really saying something."

About the Author

Nancy Krulik is the author of more than 150 books for children and young adults, including three *New York Times* Best Sellers and the popular Katie Kazoo, Switcheroo books. She lives in New York City with her family, and many of George Brown's escapades are based on things her own kids have done. (No one delivers a good burp quite like Nancy's son, Ian!) Nancy's favorite thing to do is laugh, which comes in pretty handy when you're trying to write funny books! You can follow Nancy on Twitter: @NancyKrulik.

About the Illustrator

Aaron Blecha was raised by a school of giant squid in Wisconsin and now lives with his family by the south English seaside. He works as an artist designing funny characters and illustrating humorous books, including the one you're holding. You can enjoy more of his weird creations at www.monstersquid.com.